KT-153-747

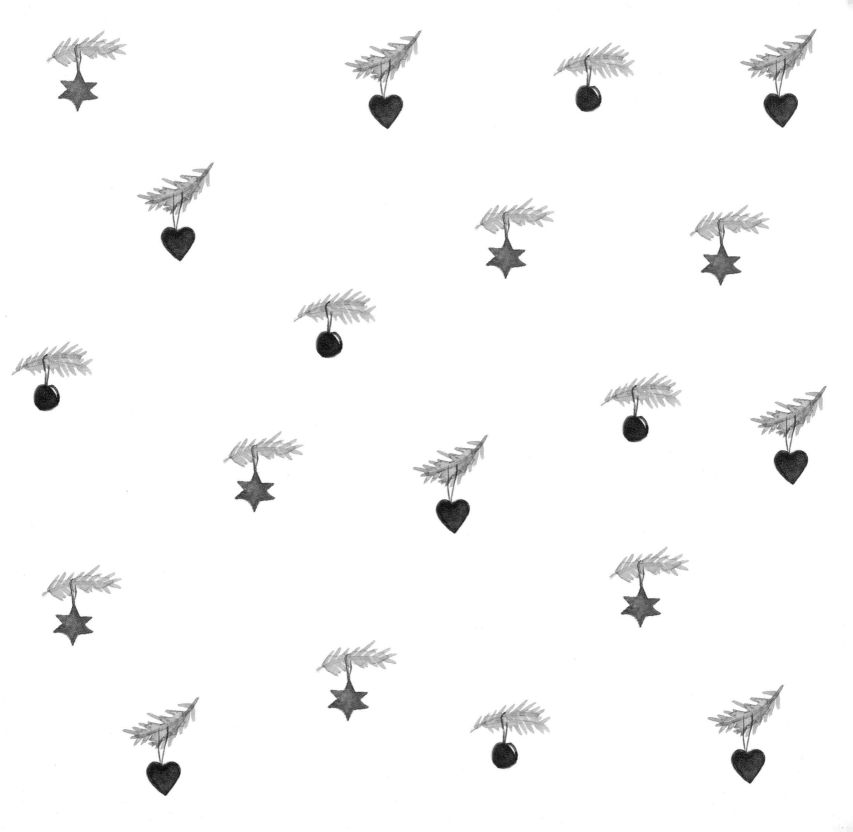

British Library Cataloguing in Publication Data
A catalogue record for this book is available from the British Library.

ISBN 0 340 85417 0 Hardback
ISBN 0 340 85418 9 Paperback

Text and illustrations copyright © Deborah Inkpen 2002

The right of Deborah Inkpen to be identified as the author and illustrator
of this Work has been asserted by her in accordance with
the Copyright, Designs and Patents Act 1988.

10 9 8 7 6 5 4 3 2 1

First published 2002
by Hodder Children's Books
a division of Hodder Headline Limited
338 Euston Road London NW1 3BH

Printed in Hong Kong

All rights reserved

HARRIET
AND THE LITTLE FAT FAIRY

DEBORAH INKPEN

*Hodder
Children's
Books*

A division of Hodder Headline Limited

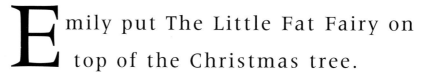

Emily put The Little Fat Fairy on
top of the Christmas tree.
'Now, don't fall off again!' she said.
The fairy smiled blankly.
Emily jumped down from the
chair and ran to Harriet's
cage. She lifted the
little hamster gently from
her nest.
'It's Christmas Eve,'
she whispered.

Emily took her over to the Christmas tree.

'Look,' she said stretching out her hand.

Harriet opened one eye. A huge, dark, spiky shape towered above her. It was covered in hundreds of fairy lights. They seemed to dance and twinkle all around her.

Harriet sniffed the air. It smelled of pine trees.

She crawled to the end of Emily's hand.
The pine needles prickled her nose.
She stretched a little further, lost her
balance and fell, landing upside down on one of
the branches.

Emily giggled. 'You don't make a
very good Christmas decoration,'
she said. She took some tinsel and
popped it on Harriet's head.

'That's better,' said Emily.

Harriet's tinsel floated to the floor. Emily caught it. When she looked up, Harriet had gone.

'Oh, no!' said Emily.

She peered into the branches. She could just make out Harriet's little pink nose. She dived under the tree, searching desperately through the maze of prickly branches and Christmas decorations.

Harriet had disappeared.

At the top of the tree
The Little Fat Fairy
continued to smile.

H arriet began to explore her sparkly,
new world. She peered into a shiny,
gold bauble. A funny little face peered back.

S he tried nibbling a red
plastic berry.
It was hard and tasteless.

Then she nibbled a
chocolate snowman.
That tasted better, once
she had chewed past the
silver paper.

Emily's brother Billy came to help.

They caught glimpses of Harriet, scampering through the branches but always just out of reach.

After a while they lost sight of her altogether. They sat down, their hands scratched and sore.

'She's probably left the tree by now,' said Billy. 'She could be anywhere!'

Emily looked tearful.

'Let's put her cage under the Christmas tree,' he said. 'Perhaps she will find her own way home.'

Emily wrote a letter to Father Christmas. 'Dear Father Christmas, please can you bring back my hamster?'

Emily's mum warned her daughter, as she grabbed her hat and coat, that Father Christmas was very busy on Christmas Eve, and perhaps he would not have time to answer her letter.

Emily said she was sure he would. But her mother didn't hear. She had already left to go shopping.

Emily thought for a moment and then added,

'P.S. And could you bring her a friend?'

H arriet had not left the Christmas tree.
She was busily climbing through the branches
and had come across some very curious things:

A tiny straw reindeer.

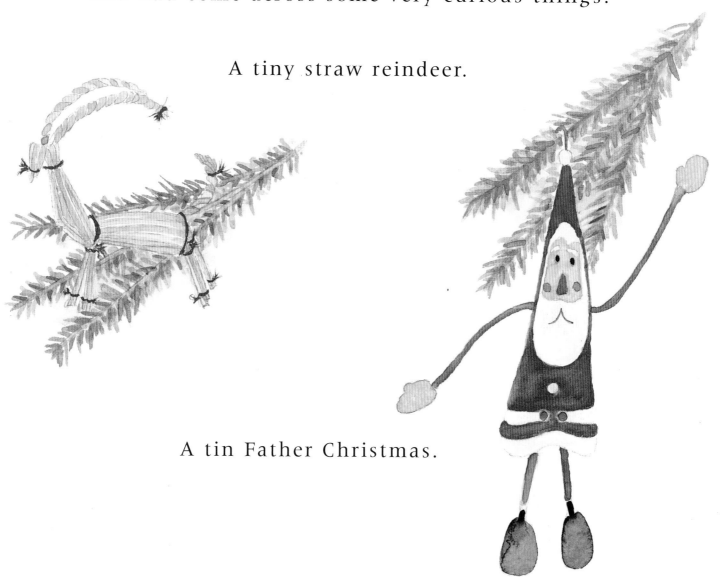

A tin Father Christmas.

A painted, cardboard
teddy bear,

and a little red basket,
which fitted her perfectly.

Emily and Billy spent the afternoon drawing until their mum returned from shopping. She was carrying a little white box with holes in the sides, which she took upstairs, before joining them for tea.

'Harriet's not back yet then?' she said. They shook their heads.

Emily had one last look under the tree before bedtime.

The cage was still empty.

'Don't worry,' said her mum, as she tucked
Emily into bed. 'I expect she will turn up.'
When she was sure that Emily and Billy were
fast asleep, Emily's mum picked up the box and
tiptoed downstairs to the Christmas tree. . .

At the top of the
Christmas tree Harriet
came face to face with The
Little Fat Fairy. As she
scrambled up on to the
fairy's shoulder, the slender
branch began to wobble.

They balanced there
for a moment, then the
fairy toppled forwards.
She tumbled down through
the branches, taking
Harriet with her.

H arriet landed with a thud on top of the fairy.

She rolled on to the floor. . .

. . .and sat up next to her cage. Curled up inside was a Russian hamster, just like herself!

Harriet lay still for a moment, just watching, wondering what to do. She tried the cage door. It was shut tight. She ran up and down the bars. There was no way in.

The Little Fat Fairy lay near by. Exhausted from her adventure, Harriet nuzzled into the fairy's soft, shimmery jumper.

As she closed her eyes she heard the sound of sleigh bells. By the time Father Christmas arrived, Harriet was fast asleep.

When Emily came down on Christmas morning, Harriet was back in her cage, and she was not alone!

'Wow!' said Billy.

'Oh, my goodness!' said Mum. 'Three hamsters!'

'Father Christmas did answer my letter!' said Emily. 'I knew he would!'

As she bent down to open the cage, Emily spotted the fairy.

'Fallen off again?' she said. The Little Fat Fairy just smiled back.

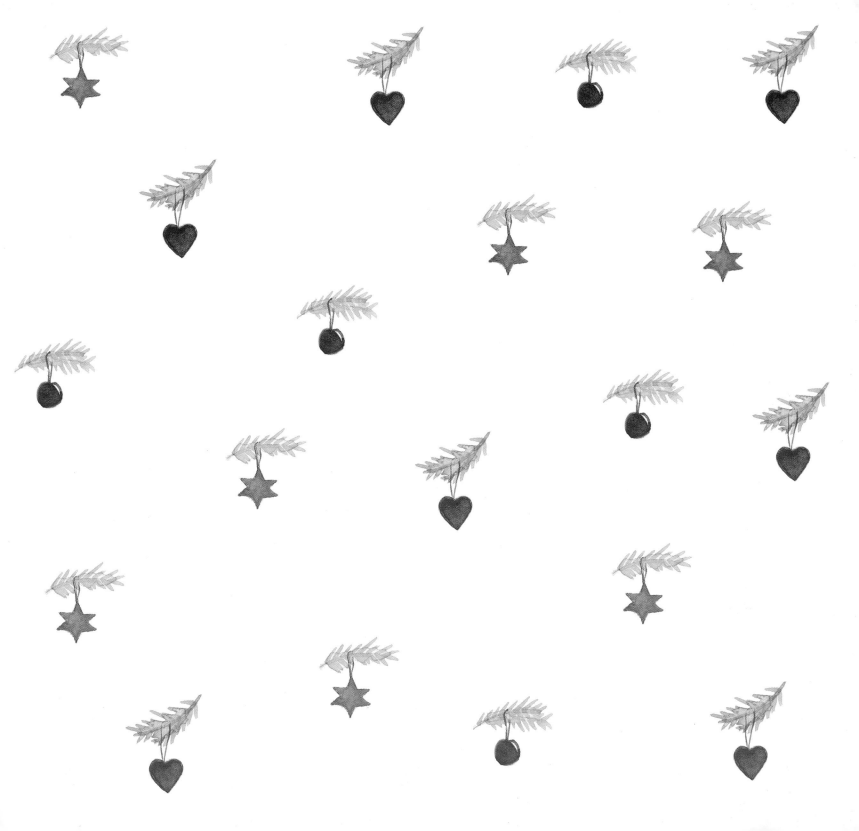